BARNYARD BOOGIE!

By Tim McCanna ◆ Illustrated by Allison Black

Abrams Appleseed
New York

The Barnyard Band is performing today.
All the musicians are ready to play!

Horse brings the tuba.

OOMPA DOOMPA DOO!

Goat swings the sax.

But what can Cow do?

But what can Cow do?

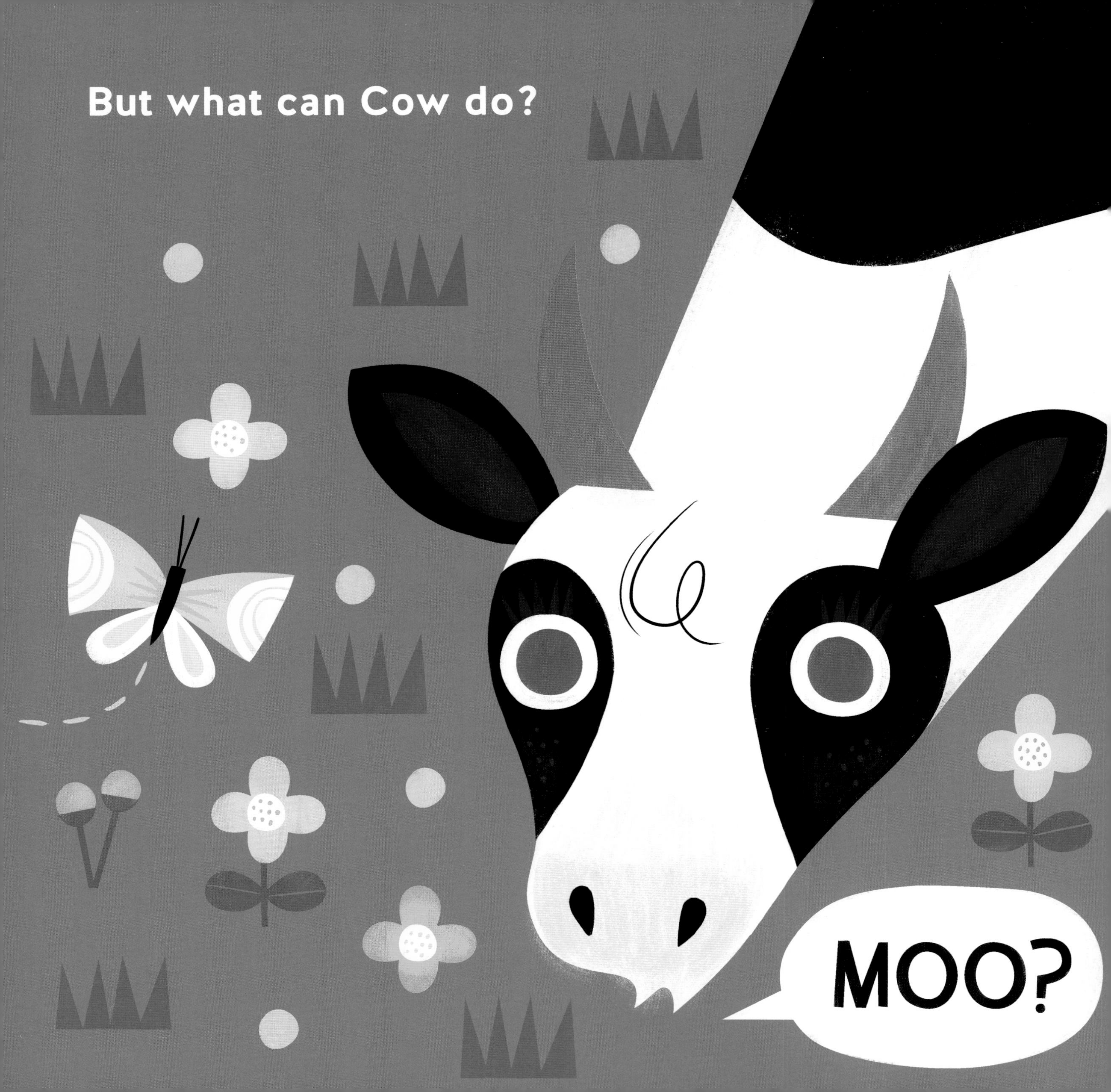

Sheep blares the trumpet.

BLATTA BLATTA BLAT!

Dog bangs the drums.

RATTA TATTA TAT!

But what can Cow do?

The crowd is waiting
to hear the show.

"How will they start?"
"When will they go?"

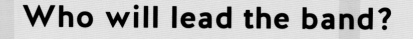

COW, of course!

Come on, let's boogie and give a hand to
Cow and the Barnyard Animal Band!

To future farmers and budding musicians everywhere.
—T.M.

For my husband, Matt, who puts the happy in my life and in my art.
—A.B.

The illustrations in this book were made digitally with Adobe Photoshop.

Cataloging-in-Publication Data has been applied for
and may be obtained from the Library of Congress.

ISBN: 978-1-4197-2346-9

Text copyright © 2017 Tim McCanna
Illustrations copyright © 2017 Allison Black
Book design by Alyssa Nassner

Printed and bound in China
10 9 8 7 6 5 4 3 2 1

For bulk discount inquiries, contact specialsales@abramsbooks.com.

ABRAMS The Art of Books
115 West 18th Street, New York, NY 10011
abramsbooks.com